Gifted From:

Gifted To:

Date:

Date I read this book myself:

The Abominable Snow Baby

Written by Daniel R. Fanelli

Illustrations by Jenna Bertino

The Abominable Snow Monster
was coming,
and the town's people were
running in fear!

As they ran they yelled:

"Help! Help!"

"He's big!"

"He's scary!"

But behind him there was

someone following him,

someone very special,

and someone very small.

It was the

Abominable Snow Baby!

"Hi! I'm the

Abominable Snow Baby.

There goes Daddy!

He's off to save the world again.

Mommy says he's going to

'worky-worky'."

"It makes me sad, very sad,
because I don't have anyone to
play with. Everybody runs!
It may be because when Daddy
walks the ground rumbles.
It may be because
Daddy is scary,
or it may be because people
think I look scary.
But the truth is, I just want to
have someone to play with,
even just one friend."

As the tear running down the
Abominable Snow Baby's
face froze, ...

... two children ran away from the Abominable Snow Baby as they yelled in fear!

Kenny yelled, "Hurry!
The monster's coming!
We've got to get out of here!"

Caitlyn yelled,
"Run, Kenny, run!
It's a monster!"

As Kenny and Caitlyn escaped

to safety, Caitlyn said,

"We are safe now!"

Then they both looked around

and frantically said

at the same time,

"Where's Kelsie?!?!

Where's Baby Kelsie?

Oh no! We left her behind!"

The town was totally deserted,
except there were two very
special babies in the town square.

One was the
Abominable Snow Baby.
He sat in front of the fountain,
sad, ... and all alone.

"Everyone is afraid of me, and
no one will be my friend."

Then Kelsie came out from behind the fountain and said, "I'm not afraid of you. I'll be your friend."

"You mean you're not afraid?" said the Abominable Snow Baby.

"No", Kelsie said, "I think you look cool, and I love to play in the snow!"

The Abominable Snow Baby and Kelsie were having so much fun playing in the snow.

The Abominable Snow Baby giggled, "I love making Snow Angels!"

Kelsie giggled back, "Me too! This is fun!"

Then suddenly, Caitlyn and Kenny ran into the town square. As they saw Kelsie, they ran toward her, and yelled, "Run, Kelsie! Run! It's a monster!"

At first, Kelsie was surprised to see Caitlyn and Kenny running toward her. Then when she heard them she said firmly,

"No! I will not run. He's not a monster. He's the Abominable Snow Baby. He's nice and he's my friend. He will not hurt you.

Plus, he likes to play in the snow, just like we do!"

Kenny and Caitlyn saw how happy
Kelsie looked when she was
playing in the snow.

They both thought about it,
and now liked the idea of having
the Abominable Snow Baby
as a new friend, too.

Caitlyn said, "Kenny, I think we
were wrong about the
Abominable Snow Baby.
Look how nice he is, and they
were definitely having fun
playing in the snow!"

Kenny said, "I agree! Let's play!"

They were all full of smiles as
they played together.
Caitlyn said to Kenny and Kelsie,

"This so much fun!

The Abominable Snow Baby

is so strong. I really like him.

We are so lucky to have

him as our friend!"

Then Kenny said to

the Abominable Snow Baby,

"You're so cool!"

The Abominable Snow Baby
had never been so happy!

"My new friends are awesome!
They actually think
I'm cool, and they are not
afraid of me.
It is so neat to have
Caitlyn and Kenny as friends.
Did you know they are twins?
And Kelsie is a baby just like me.
I love my new friends!

"See you later.
I'm going to play with my
new *Best Friends Forever!*"

The End

We hope you have enjoyed this book.
If you would like to order another copy of this book, or would like to order the Kindle
digital ebook version, please go to Amazon.com and enter

The Abominable Snow Baby
in the search window.

We would like to invite you to add your comments about this book on Amazon.com
and Facebook.com, and would like to extend a special thank you to those who take
the time to "like" The Abominable Snow Baby, or write kind comments.

For a signed copy or bulk orders, please send a written request to:

The Editor's Desk
The Abominable Snow Baby
13506 Summerport Village Pkwy, #228
Windermere, FL 34786

Email comments, questions or suggestions to:
asnowbabybook@gmail.com

The Abominable Snow Baby

Written by Daniel R. Fanelli
Illustrations by Jenna Bertino

Printed in Great Britain
by Amazon